Hamish McHaggis

This book belongs to

....

....

Publishing

www.gwpublishing.com

This is Hamish the haggis
of the McHaggis clan,
never been seen
by the eyes of man

Hamish

Rupert Harold the Third
is an English gent,
travelling far from
his home in Kent

Rupert

Our Jeannie's an osprey with wide sweeping wings,
who is easily distracted by all sorts of things

Jeannie

Angus

Young Angus is cheeky and likes playing the fool,
whatever he's doing he's got to look cool

For Elissa
with love LS

For Lesley
with love SJC

Text and illustrations copyright © Linda Strachan and Sally J. Collins

www.lindastrachan.com

First published in paperback in Great Britain 2006

The rights of Linda Strachan and Sally J. Collins to be identified
as the author and illustrator of this work have been asserted by them
in accordance with the Copyright, Designs and Patents Act 1988

Design - Veneta Hooper

Reprographics - GWP Graphics

Printing - Printer Trento, Italy

Published by

GW Publishing
PO Box 6091
Thatcham
Berks
RG19 8XZ

Tel +44 (0) 1635 268080
www.gwpublishing.com

ISBN 09551564-1-6
978-09551564-1-0

Hamish McHaggis

And

The Skirmish at Stirling

By Linda Strachan

Illustrated by Sally J. Collins

One bright morning Rupert came down the hill to the Hoggle to find Hamish dancing about with a long piece of wood in his hand and wearing a colander on his head.

"What are you doing, Hamish?" Rupert asked, trying to keep a straight face.

"I'm practising," Hamish poked the stick at a large bush. Angus scampered down the tree. "What's going on?" he asked.

"I thought we could all go to the battle re-enactment at Stirling Castle," Hamish told them.

Angus looked
confused. "What's that?"
    "A re-enactment is when you get
dressed up in costumes and act out
things that happened long ago."

With a flurry of feathers Jeannie crash-landed beside them.
"Here they are, Hamish," she gasped.

Her travelling net was full to bursting with books of all shapes and sizes and lots of coloured cloth.

"I've found these books about Scottish history. There are some about Bannockburn and the Battle of Stirling Bridge and of course William Wallace. *My hero!*" she giggled.

"I could be the King of England, Edward II, at Bannockburn," Rupert said, pointing to a picture in Jeannie's book.

"Don't you want to be on our side, Rupert?" asked Angus. "Don't you want to be friends with us anymore?"

"It's just pretend, Angus," Hamish told him. "Rupert is always going to be our friend."

"Of course I will, Angus," Rupert promised him. "It's just a bit of fun."

"I could take a sword and I'll
make a special shield, too."

"I'll take my picnic basket and I want
to make a proper helmet, just like the ones
they used to wear. I could use this!"

"We need a flag for the Whirry Bang. The Saltire is blue and white. I can make that."

"I must remember to take my new camera and perhaps I could take my bagpipes, too?"

The next day Hamish was decorating the Whirry Bang. "I think it should look a bit like a battle wagon, with shields," he said.
"Can we put a string of coloured flags on it?" suggested Angus.

"That's what I thought, Angus. I made some bunting this morning." Jeannie pulled it out of her net to show him.

"That's magic! It could go here, and here!" Angus grinned as he looped the flags around Jeannie's wings.

"Angus!" Jeannie tried to move but she was all tangled up.

"Sorry, Jeannie," Angus giggled. "But you look so funny like that. Stay still a moment and I'll help you get loose."

Angus unwound the string and Jeannie helped him tie the flags on to the Whirry Bang.

They set off for Stirling Castle early the next morning. Jeannie was excited, she couldn't wait to tell everyone what she had read in her history book. "Do you know how the Saltire became the Scottish flag?"

She peered down from the roof of the Whirry Bang. "St Andrew is the patron saint of Scotland and a very long time ago, in 832AD, King Angus and the Scots were surrounded by a much bigger army."

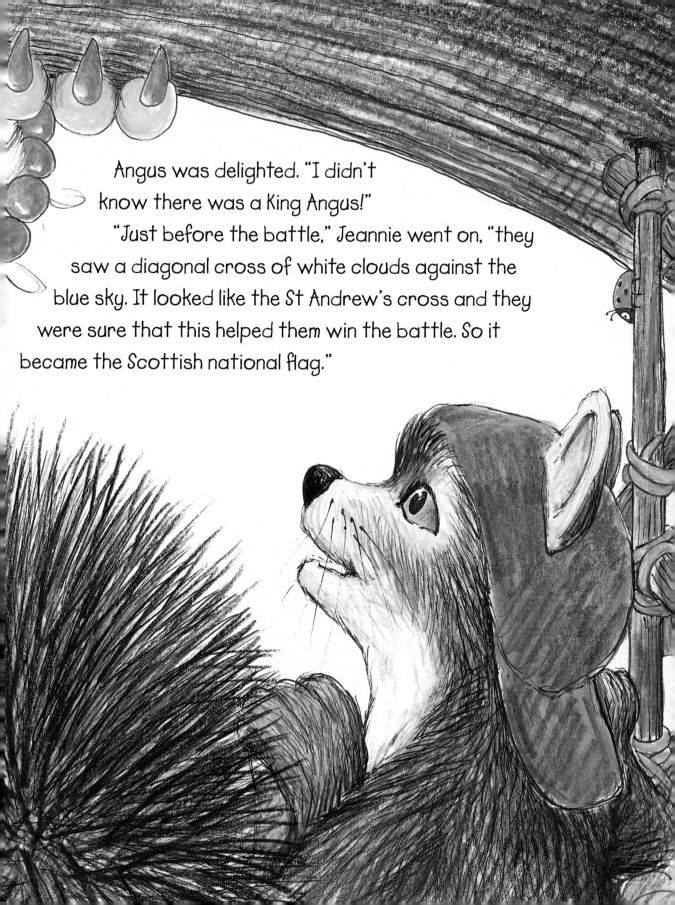

Angus was delighted. "I didn't know there was a King Angus!"

"Just before the battle," Jeannie went on, "they saw a diagonal cross of white clouds against the blue sky. It looked like the St Andrew's cross and they were sure that this helped them win the battle. So it became the Scottish national flag."

"Wait! What's that, Hamish? Hey, stop!" shouted Rupert. "Look, over there!"

"What're you jibberin on aboot?" Hamish grumbled. "You nearly made me crash the Whirry Bang."

"There's something over there, on that hedge," Rupert said, jumping out and running across the heather.

Snagged on a prickly bramble was a piece of red and yellow cloth. Rupert tugged it loose.

"It's a flag. The Lion Rampant," Jeannie told him, as Rupert held it up. "That's Scotland's other flag! Perhaps someone dropped it on their way to the castle. We could take it with us and see if we can find out who it belongs to."

When they arrived at Stirling Castle they drove the Whirry Bang through the castle entrance and into the Queen Anne Gardens where there were lots of people dressed up in costume. Jeannie noticed a little boy looking very sad.

"I've lost my flag," he sniffed.

"It must have blown away on the road," his *mum* told him.

Jeannie realised it was the Lion Rampant that they had found on their way to the castle. "Is that your flag?" she asked.

"Oh, yes, it is!" the boy said, with a huge smile. "Thank you!"

"Look Angus," said Hamish. "They're about to do a battle display. Let's go and watch them." They went up onto the walls above the gardens, to get a good view.

"That muckle one is William Wallace," Hamish pointed to the bigger of the two men. "And the other one must be an English knight!"

"Look at the swords and shields," said Rupert, frowning. "I don't know if I would like to wear a helmet like that!"

The clash of swords on wooden shields announced the start of the battle. It was very exciting and Angus was soon leaping about shouting for one side or the other.

After the display Rupert suggested that they stage their own version of the Battle of Bannockburn.

"I'm King Edward of England," Rupert declared, showing off his shield.

"I'm Robert the Bruce of Scotland," Hamish retaliated, "and I'm going to win!" Hamish and Rupert ran towards each other waving swords and shields.

Clank!
Clunk!

"I'm on the English side with you, Rupert!" Jeannie squawked, as she dropped a water bag on top of Angus.

"Jeannie! I'm wringing wet!" Angus laughed and waved his sword at her. "Oops, sorry!" Jeannie shrieked, as she flew past again. "I really meant to miss you, Angus."

Splat!

Suddenly Rupert fell over and lay still on the ground. Hamish stared at him. He wasn't moving at all.

But Hamish wasn't convinced. "Did you dunt yer heid?" he asked Rupert. "I didn't even touch you!"

"What's wrong, Rupert?" Angus came rushing over. "Are you hurt? What happened?" Jeannie skidded on the grass and almost collided with them. "What is it? Why is Rupert not getting up?"

Hamish was suspicious and just then Rupert started to shake. He was laughing. "I just tripped. I was pretending to be wounded."

Hamish laughed when he saw Angus. "Look at you, Angus, you're drookit! I think it's time for a picnic!"

They found a good spot for their picnic and they were just
in time. An announcement came over the loudspeaker.

"It is time to award the prizes for the best costumes of
the day and we have a special prize for this wonderfully
decorated battle wagon."

"He means the Whirry Bang!" Angus squealed,
jumping up and down.

Hamish went up and collected the prize. "This is beezer!" he grinned as he showed them the special cup, a Scottish quaich. But Angus was hungry. "Look, Jeannie, there are oatcakes and lots of lovely cheese, fresh raspberries and even some bannocks. We can have a great picnic!"

It was almost dark by the time they set off
back to Coorie Doon in the Whirry Bang
battle wagon with the Saltire still flying
proudly at the back.

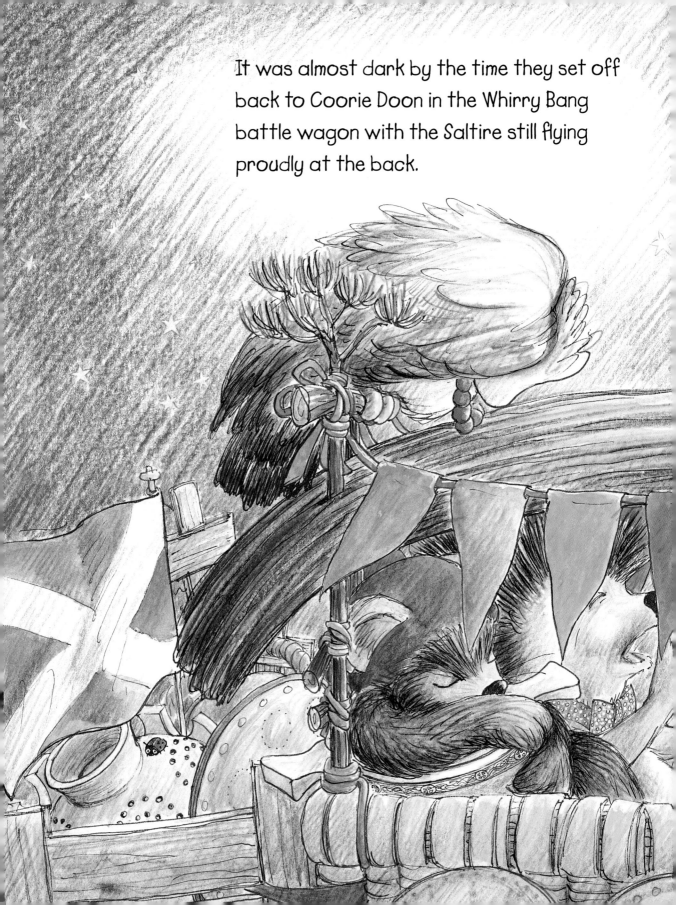

On the way home Jeannie tucked her head under her wing and Angus fell asleep, cuddling the quaich they had won.

"It's been a grand day," said Rupert, yawning.

"Aye," agreed Hamish. "It was that."

Bang!
Whirr!

DID YOU KNOW?

Coorie Doon means to nestle or cosy down comfortably

Blether means to gossip or chatter

Dunt yer heid means to bang your head

That's magic/Beezer means something is excellent or great

Muckle means big or large

Drookit means soaking wet

What're you jibberin on aboot? means what are you chattering about

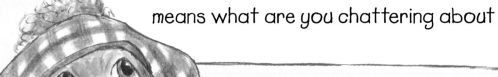

Haggis. It is commonly thought that a Haggis has three legs, two long and one short. Hamish often wonders who thought that one up!

Angus is a Pine Marten.

Pine Martens sometimes steal food from bird tables. They love jam sandwiches.

Hedgehogs sometimes snore and they also appear to dream, snorting and chirping quietly in their sleep.

Ospreys have been known to build their nests on telephone poles.

The Quaich is a two-handed Scottish traditional drinking vessel, 'the cup of welcome'.

A man tried to fly from **Stirling Castle** in 1507, with a pair of wings made from chicken feathers. He ended up in the mud – splat!

Other books in the series

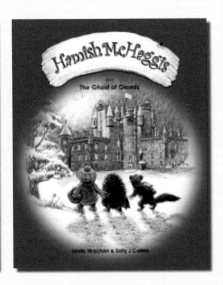

Hamish McHaggis and The Edinburgh Adventure

Hamish has tickets for the Tattoo at Edinburgh Castle, but will they make it?
09546701-7-5

Hamish McHaggis and The Search for The Loch Ness Monster

Rupert doesn't believe in the Loch Ness Monster, so Hamish and his friends take him to find Nessie.
09546701-5-9

Hamish McHaggis and The Ghost of Glamis

Angus hears scary noises when they visit Hamish's grandfather at Glamis Castle, could it be a ghost?
09546701-9-1

By the same author/illustrator

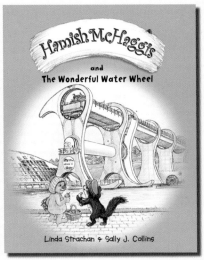

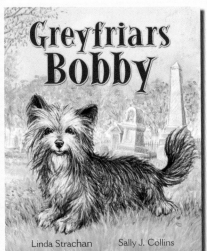

Hamish McHaggis and The Skye Surprise

Jeannie's brother is having a surprise party on the Isle of Skye, but he's not the only one who gets a surprise.
09546701-8-3

Hamish McHaggis and The Wonderful Water Wheel

Angus is having trouble with his boats but a trip on the canal to the Falkirk Wheel gives him an idea.
09551564-0-8
978-09551564-0-3

Greyfriars Bobby

The little dog whose loyalty to his master made him a legend.
09551564-2-4
978-09551564-2-7